Might goes hand in hand with right as He-Man and the Masters of the Universe fight to make their planet safe. The greatest of their enemies is Skeletor, the Lord of Destruction, and his evil band, whose hatred for their foes is never-ending. The war goes on but who will win?

First edition

© LADYBIRD BOOKS LTD MCMLXXXIV and MATTEL INC MCMLXXXIV

Castle Grayskull Under Attack!

by John Grant

illustrated by Robin Davies

Ladybird Books Loughborough

In his lair in the heart of Snake Mountain
Skeletor, Lord of Destruction, eagerly studied an
ancient stone tablet. His eyes blazed as he read
the carved letters. "At last!" he cried in
triumph. "The secret of the ancient Eternians. I
will tap the power of the planet itself. Not all
the strength of Castle Grayskull can stop me."

In the sulphurous cavern below the mountain, Skeletor put his slaves the Skelcons to work to construct a machine which would tap the power of Eternia and convert it to energy of untold strength. Under the threat of their lord's energy-blade, the Skelcons quickly completed their task ... a mammoth power-shield projector. Towering on its three telescopic legs, Skeletor's creation gleamed in the glare of the Skelcons' forge.

"Now we shall see who rules Eternia!" cried Skeletor, as the Skelcons swarmed over the machine to prepare it for action.

5

Far from Snake Mountain, in a wide clearing of the Evergreen Forest, stood Castle Grayskull. The grim battlements dominated the land for many leagues round, as far as the hills which rimmed the clearing and the beginning of the forest.

In the castle's Council Chamber, Teela and Stratos, Lord of the Air, were in deep discussion. Only by constant vigilance were the two able to hold at bay the forces of evil which daily threatened the people of Eternia, for He-Man was away and could not help.

They were especially worried over a report by Stratos that swarms of Sea-People led by their lord, Mer-Man, were making their way towards the mouth of the River Doom. The river flowed near Castle Grayskull, and it was not in the nature of Mer-Man to pay friendly calls.

Making a powerful video-lens with his energy-blade, Skeletor spied on the Council Chamber just as Teela sent out a call for He-Man to come to their aid. "Let him come!" he snarled. "They and their precious castle are finished."

Skeletor now summoned his ally, Mer-Man, to assemble with his army of Sea-People beyond the hills where the River Doom flowed out through a narrow gorge. And while they swam and slithered and squelched their way upstream, the Skelcons dragged Skeletor's power-shield projector overland to the meeting place. The red sun of Eternia was setting when Skeletor stood on a hilltop and gazed towards the castle. A few lights showed in the gathering dusk, and after a time they went out.

"Sleep sound," laughed Skeletor. "Against the swarming hordes of the ocean you have no chance, for I will create an ocean just for them, to bring them to your very threshold. And you need not think that all your clever toys will be of the slightest help. I have the power to stop any mechanical device."

Under cover of darkness the Skelcons started to set up the projector beside the river where the hills would hide it from the castle ... until it was too late.

In his other guise of the weakling Prince Adam, He-Man was at the Palace of Eternia, talking to his mother, the Queen. When Teela's cry for help reached him, he left the palace and raised his sword. "By the power of Grayskull!" he cried — and became He-Man. Within minutes he was with his friends at the castle.

Just before dawn, the Skelcons got the power-shield projector into position. The probe was poised to drill down through the planet's crust to the energy core far below. A final check and the machine hummed into life. The twisting probe drilled into the rock. The tripod vibrated with energy. And the projector module on top began to glow with flickering light.

The projector module rose on its elevator stem until it topped the hills. Nothing lay between it and Castle Grayskull. The glow of the projector pulsations increased, and waves of power sped invisibly out to ring the castle. Within a few moments Castle Grayskull was enclosed in an unseen bubble of power.

"Now for the second part of my plan," gloated Skeletor.

At his command a slimy band of Sea-People led by Mer-Man emerged from the river, each carrying a zero-energy weapon.

At the spot where the River Doom flowed into the gorge, Mer-Man stationed his Sea-People. Then at a signal, each aimed his zero-energy weapon at the water. Brilliant green bolts of zero energy flashed from the weapons, and ice crystals began to form in the water, slowing its flow and then stopping it completely as it froze from side to side. As the water piled up behind the ice, the Sea-People poured more and more

and more zero energy into the river until a huge
ice dam filled the gorge from one side to the
other.

Upstream the river water rose above its banks
and flooded on to the land. Soon the river itself
was out of sight, and the waters lapped about
the very walls of Castle Grayskull.

Now the creatures of the ocean
swarmed through the flood, ready
to seize any living thing that
might try to escape from
the castle.

He-Man was roused from sleep by the cry of a lookout. Hurrying to the ramparts he looked where the man pointed. But it was still dark, and there was nothing to see.

"I heard a sound," said the sentry. "It wasn't a footstep. It wasn't a wheel. It seemed to come from all sides at once."

As the sun rose, and light poured over the landscape, it became plain that this was no ordinary attack by an enemy over land. The lapping waters were filled with every kind of sea horror, ready to attack with teeth, claws and tentacles.

He-Man leapt into Battle-Ram, but the controls clicked uselessly. His power-blade was dead, as was Teela's power-sceptre.

"With my super-strength I might just fight my way through to dry land," said He-Man. "But the ordinary people of the castle would be helpless. Already the water has reached the jawbridge. Unless we can find a way of fighting back before the water rises much further, we are doomed."

At noon the water reached half-way up the walls of Castle Grayskull. Only the jawbridge, held tight by its neutralised mechanism, kept the flood from entering. Evil sea creatures clawed at the stones and reached up with writhing tentacles.

"We are in the grip of some kind of power-shield," said He-Man. "Everything mechanical is jammed, but *we* are not affected. And the enemy can penetrate right up to our walls. If there was a way, a man could also break through and seek help."

"If only we had weapons that used natural power," said Teela.

"Man-at-Arms might devise something," said Stratos. "The power-shield may not extend overhead. If I can penetrate it, I can bring help."

Without another word, Stratos soared straight up from the ramparts, braced for impact with the power-shield.

For an instant Stratos was enclosed by a blue glow. A sharp electrical tingle went through his body. Then he was through the power-shield and into the open sky. Far below was the helpless castle. But farther off he could now see the great ice dam that held back the waters of the River Doom.

High above Eternia, a mere speck in the sky and unnoticed by Skeletor and his people, Stratos sped with all the air-power he could

summon up to find Man-at-Arms, armourer to
the Masters of the Universe.

The sun was low in the sky when Stratos
spiralled to the ground at the Palace of Eternia.
Man-at-Arms came to greet him, and he spoke
his urgent message. Castle Grayskull was under
siege and only Man-at-Arms could save it.

When Stratos had finished his story, Man-at-Arms looked thoughtful. "Whatever weapon I can devise for Castle Grayskull must not rely on mechanical power. It must be done swiftly before the waters rise much more. And it must be done secretly so that the enemy has no time to produce a counter weapon."

"The sun shone through the power-shield," said Stratos.

"Of course," cried Man-at-Arms. "Solar

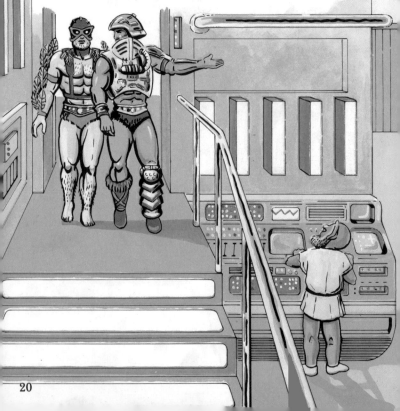

energy. It requires no mechanism. And you say
that Skeletor has blocked the river with a great
mass of ice. Then, we'll use a solar cannon. As
long as the sun shines it will be all-powerful.
Now, you must rest. And I and my people have
much work to do."

At a touch, the wall at the back of the room
slid silently to one side, revealing the entrance to
the workshop where Man-at-Arms and his
servants, the Nerlins, produced incredible
weapon systems.

All that night, the following day, and well into the next evening the Nerlins laboured under the guidance of Man-at-Arms.

From bronze they fashioned a great cup-shaped mirror, polished to a dazzling brilliance to catch every ray of sunlight.

They quarried masses of quartz from the mountain which would filter the sun's rays and extract the last particle of energy.

And from deep in the underground caves of Eternia the Nerlins brought dazzling pieces of crystal to form the lenses which would direct the power of the sun on to its target.

All this Stratos watched with awe, but conscious all the time that the waters were still inching their way up the defences of Castle Grayskull. He watched as the Nerlins completed the assembly of the solar cannon. Then the cannon was hoisted up to hang below Man-at-Arms' hovering wind raider.

In darkness the wind raider rose swiftly and headed for Castle Grayskull. As the image of the castle grew on the video-nav screen, Man-at-Arms reduced speed until the wind raider hovered directly above. While he lowered the cargo winch cable, Stratos spiralled down, through the power-shield, and was soon standing on the ramparts. Quickly he explained to He-Man and Teela what must be done.

Slowly the solar cannon was lowered to the defenders, while the wind raider hovered unaffected by Skeletor's power-shield. Once the cannon was down it was moved into place until at last it stood poised on the battlements of Castle Grayskull. There was nothing to do now but wait. And pray that the sun would not be obscured by cloud.

From a vantage point on the surrounding hills, Skeletor viewed the strange construction which had appeared overnight on the top of Castle Grayskull.

"The poor misguided fools," he sneered. "What puny weapon can hope to overcome the power of planet Eternia? Another few hours and they will be forced to choose between drowning and capture by my sea slaves."

Figures could be seen grouped around the cannon. Then a bolt of white hot solar energy shot from it. It struck the water in front of Skeletor, throwing up a cloud of super-heated steam. A second bolt plunged into the hillside above the ice dam. Skeletor watched the burst of smoke and flame from the scorched undergrowth.

"Increase power!" he screamed at the Skelcon operators of the power-shield projector. And the machine throbbed and trembled as Skeletor attempted to reinforce the power-shield around the castle.

The flood waters had now risen so high that the defenders of Castle Grayskull were forced to use swords and spears to repel the grasping tentacles and snapping jaws of the sea creatures. With Teela at the controls of the solar cannon, Stratos hovered high in the sky to direct her shots.

The first bolt of solar power fell short. The second was too high. At Stratos' signals, Teela changed the aim and swung the cannon a few degrees to the right. Then she pressed the firing lever.

Far off, in the gap in the hills, there shot up a cloud of white vapour. Teela fired again, with the same result.

Stratos signalled her to maintain rapid fire, then he swooped down, sword in hand, to help to beat off the attackers.

The first few shots from the solar cannon seemed to have no effect on the ice. But Skeletor ordered the power-shield to be still further strengthened. The terrified Skelcons did as they were told, and the projector shook violently, glowing and smoking at maximum power. Then Mer-Man shrieked: "The ice! It's melting!"

Water was pouring down the jumbled mass. A large chunk fell clear and crashed into the river

bed. Already a sizeable stream was pouring
out of the crevices in the ice.

And still, relentlessly, the bolts of solar energy
continued to blast into the dam. Mer-Man and
the Sea-People trained their zero-energy
weapons on the ice and fired until the power
cells were exhausted. But the ice continued to
dissolve before their eyes. Throwing down the
useless weapons, the Sea-People began
retreating, anxious to get away from the super-
heat of solar power and back to the cool wetness
of the sea.

At Stratos' signal, Teela sent one last solar
energy bolt crashing into the tottering ice dam,
and with a roar it collapsed. The freed flood
water surged through the gorge, while tumbling
blocks of shattered ice carried destruction before
them.

Skeletor's Skelcons scrambled as best they
could out of the path of the cataract. The
fleeing Sea-People found themselves overtaken
by the water and hastened even faster than they
had imagined downstream towards the sea.

Skeletor raged helplessly as water, ice and debris crashed around the slender legs of the power projector, causing it to sway alarmingly. Ignoring warning bolts from their master's energy-blade, the Skelcon operators leapt to safety as the machine toppled and vanished in a blaze of sparking electricity below the flood.

As the power-shield projector crashed into the water, the power-shield around Castle Grayskull was broken. Energy systems hummed into life. And not a moment too soon as the sea creatures prepared for their final assault. But now the water level was dropping rapidly. The attackers found themselves in danger of being stranded as the flood rolled back swiftly to the river.

Soon, the level had fallen sufficiently for the jawbridge to be lowered. Out of the gate swept Battle-Ram, skimming the surface and with bursts from its laser cannon hurrying the retreating enemy on their way.

And as the sea creatures flopped and squirmed through the shallow water to the river, Stratos joined He-Man and Battle-Ram in harrying them. While Teela, mounted on her golden horse, clattered over the jawbridge and splashed through the puddles to join in the pursuit.

From his vantage point in the sky, Stratos looked down upon the shambles where the ice dam had broken. A raging Skeletor waded in the mud and debris where the power-shield projector lay half buried. Deserted by his slaves and allies, he wrestled in vain to drag the machine upright. But even the great strength and will power of the Lord of Destruction availed him nothing against the dead weight of the metal and the clutch of the liquid ooze.

Mer-Man had been skulking among the
undergrowth, and now he emerged, hoping to
make his escape before the avenging He-Man
arrived. But Skeletor saw him.

"Miserable coward!" he raged at his ally.
"Perhaps even the feeble strength of your slimy
muscles might be enough to help me."

"I'll have no more part in it," said Mer-Man.
"The vengeance of the Masters of the Universe is
close. And it will be swift and terrible."

"Traitor!" screamed Skeletor, and from his energy-blade darted a blast of fire. Mer-Man side-stepped the bolt and aimed his own weapon. But, drained by Mer-Man's attempts to reinforce the crumbling ice dam, the weapon flickered briefly and went dead. Hurling it at Skeletor, Mer-Man made a dash for the river. Then he caught his foot on part of the projector, and sprawled in the mud as another blast from Skeletor sizzled over his head.

Before he could fire again, a voice called from the hill above. "Skeletor, throw down your weapon. Your evil plan has failed."

Skeletor spun round to face this new enemy... and lost his footing in the slime. The energy-blade flew from his grip as he went down, arcing through the air to crash into the battered projector module of the fallen machine. A white-hot disintegrating blast completed the destruction of the device as the impact triggered the energy-blade.

Slowly the smoke cleared, and He-Man looked down on the scene below him. Of the power-shield projector, there was no sign but a smoking crater on the river bank.

Mer-Man was already making good his escape downstream as Skeletor picked himself up, momentarily dazed. Weaponless, he raged after the fleeing Mer-Man. "Treacherous wretch," he screamed. "There is not one of your kind worthy of my leadership. I, Skeletor, Lord of

Destruction, am served by fools and weaklings. By your bungling and cowardice you have dared to betray me!"

"Not I," called back Mer-Man from a safe distance, "but the powers of the sky. An hour ago the storm clouds would have made the Masters' weapon useless."

As he spoke, the sun was already disappearing behind a thick cloudbank.

After many days of skulking, weaponless, from one refuge to another, Skeletor reached the safety of Snake Mountain and his lair behind the Blood Falls. For long days and nights he brooded on the failure of his scheme, and his slaves avoided him in terror of his maniacal rage. Even the ferocious Panthor, Skeletor's giant feline, cringed in a corner of the cavern.

Then, one morning Skeletor roused himself. Gathering the ancient slab on which were inscribed the secrets of the power of planet Eternia, he mounted Panthor and rode swiftly across the bridge towards the smouldering volcanic crater of the opposite peak.

"So much for the wisdom of the ancient Eternians," he roared. "The ancient Eternians were fools!"

And he hurled the graven stone into the fiery depths.

Back at Castle Grayskull the Masters watched Skeletor's action on the spy-scan monitor.

"The fools," said Teela, "are not the discoverers of wisdom, but those like Skeletor who try to put it to evil use."